Ratman and the Big Cat

Clive Gifford

Illustrated by Rikki O'Neill

"**D**ad! Dad! It is very bad!"
Dad put down his pen
and ran into the kitchen.
Sam and Jan looked sad.

"What's wrong?" asked Dad.

"My red **jam** has gone," said Sam.
"I hid it by the pans."

"And so has my **ham**," said Jan.

This alphabet has lost some of its letters. They were found hiding in a big bag!

Can you put the letters back in their right place in the alphabet?

y c n t g
w e q k

a b _ d _ f _ h i

j _ l m _ o p _ r

s _ u v _ x _ _ z

Dad looked at where the jam and ham should be.
"Grrrrr. This makes me mad," said Dad.

"I bet a big pig or a fat cat did this."
"A pig or a cat? Should I get the vet?" asked Jan.

"No," said Dad.
"This is not a job
for a vet.
If it is a big cat then this
is a job for.....Ratman!"

Jam and ham are words that rhyme with each other.

Can you draw a line between the words that rhyme below?

bag

hat

get

led

bar

sad

hen

pea

car

fed

tea

men

sat

rag

lad

let

Dad ran out of the house and into his van. He slammed the van's doors. WHAM! The van span and span. It span round ten times just like a fan.

Sam and Jan hid by the window and watched the van.

Out of it sprang a very strange rat.
Or was it Dad?
Sam didn't know.
It had Dad's nose and tail.
But it wore a long cloak and red cap.

"I get it!" cried Jan. "Dad has become Ratman!"

Can you change the first letter of each of the words so that they match one of the pictures? Then write the new word.

red _____ _____ _____

far _____ _____ _____

cap _____ _____ _____

met _____ _____ _____

fun _____ _____ _____

log _____ _____ _____

man _____ _____ _____

pig _____ _____ _____

"I am Ratman and I fight all that is bad.
I will trap the big cat with my net.
My rat nose tells me that this trail of wet jam
will lead me to the big cat. I bet he is in the den."

"What if **you** get hit or trapped?" asked Sam.
Ratman tapped the top of his cap.
"My magic hat will see to that."

Ratman tracked the trail of wet jam.
It led into the den where a big cat stood.

See if you can copy out these letters three times each on the lines beside them.

a _____ _____ _____

e _____ _____ _____

h _____ _____ _____

r _____ _____ _____

t _____ _____ _____

b _____ _____ _____

i _____ _____ _____

m _____ _____ _____

"**S**it!" said Ratman to the big cat. The big cat sat, but ate the last bit of ham.

"Do you know who I am?" asked Ratman.
"Are you a bat?" asked the big cat.
"No, I am Ratman. And you have been bad.
How could you eat Sam's jam and Jan's ham?"

"Easily," said the big cat.
"No one hid the ham.
And I bit through the lid of the jar of jam."

The letters in these bowls of soup are all mixed up. Can you put them in their correct order in the alphabet?

Write them in the space below each bowl.

"You had better let me get out of here," said the big cat. "I am **ten** times too big for you to hit. I've eaten, feel fat and now want a nap."

"But I am Ratman and I hit big pigs, who take food from kids."

"Well, I am a big cat...and cats **EAT** rats."

The big cat smiled.

Ratman started to fret.
The back of his neck was hot and wet.

Can you draw a line from each of these words to match the picture of yummy food?

pie

bun

cake

peas

eggs

apple

bread

chips

sweets

The big cat batted the hat off Ratman's head. He bit through the rim and then ate all the hat. Ratman bit his lip.

Without his magic hat, he was not Ratman. He was just Dad.

"N...n...nice cat," he said and gave it a pat. "We'll say no more about the ham or the jam."

"Too late," growled the big cat. "I do not like pats. They make me mad."

Say the words **pat**, **can** and **map**. Listen to the sound that the letter **a** makes in the middle of the words.

Now see if you can spot and <u>underline</u> the words in each sentence which have that sound in them.

1. "I hid it by the pans."

2. "They make me mad."

3. Dad bit back, then hit the cat.

4. It span round ten times just like a fan.

5. Sam and Jan looked sad.

6. "Dad! Dad! It is very bad!"

7. Out of it sprang a very strange rat.

8. He slammed the van's doors.

Dad and the big cat
started to battle.

WHAM! BAM!
The big cat bit Dad. "Ouch! That is not fair."

Dad bit back,
then hit the cat.
The big cat hit Dad
with a slap.

WHACK!

As Dad fell back, his net
got caught on the TV set.
He let go of the net as he
fell onto his back.

"Ow! My head," he said.
His net was now wrapped around the TV set.

Here are some other animals.

Can you match their names to the correct picture and write their names next to them?

— — — — — — — dog

— — — cow

d o g

bat

lion

fox

bear

hippo

pig

Things looked **bad**. Dad was trapped.
The big cat stood over him. He licked his lips.

Dad looked at his net caught on the TV set.
In a flash, he grabbed the net with his hand.
The TV set fell and hit the big cat.

WHACK!

SPLAT!

Even without his magic hat,
Dad was really still Ratman!
Ratman stepped back. The big cat was now flat.

All the following words are missing either a letter a or a letter o.

Can you work out which letter to add to make the word?

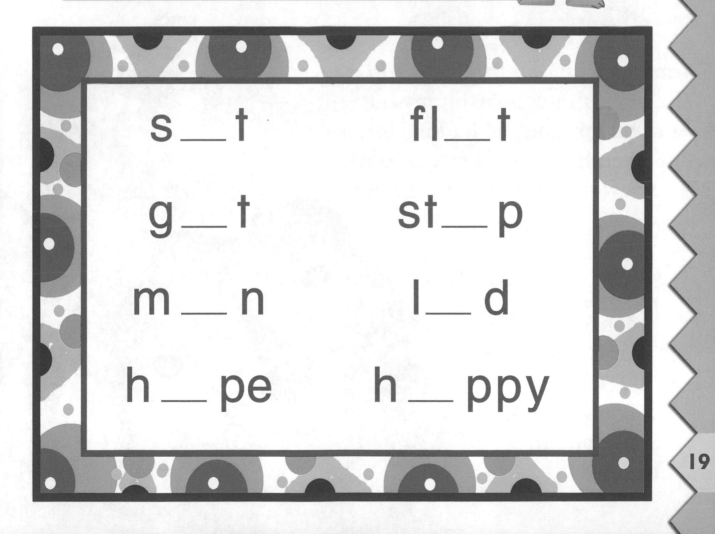

s__t   fl__t

g__t   st__p

m__n   l__d

h__pe   h__ppy

Ratman called Jan and Sam into the den.
"You can now get the vet, but let me sing my rap."

"Hit it!

I am Ratman and this is my rap.
The big cat may have bit my hat.
And thought that he had me trapped.
But when he bit me, I just hit back.
And now the big cat is flat not fat!"

The big cat groaned. "A TV set. That is not fair." "Tell that to the vet," said Ratman. Sam and Jan clapped.

Can you remember the story of Ratman and the Big Cat and answer these questions? Write them down as neatly as you can.

 What did Ratman wear on his head?

_____

 2 Whose ham was eaten by the big cat?

_____

3 What colour was the jam that the big cat ate?

_____

4 What span round ten times?

_____

5 Who ate Ratman's magic hat?

_____

 6 Did pats, nets or hats make the big cat mad?

_____

Answers

Page 3

a b **c** d **e** f **g** h i j **k** l m
n o p **q** r s **t** u v **w** x **y** z

Page 5

bag – rag   bar – car

hat – sat   sad – lad

get – let   hen – men

led – fed   pea – tea

Page 7

red   bed   fun   sun

far   car   log   dog

cap   tap   man   fan

met   net   pig   wig

Page 9

a	*a*	*a*	*a*
e	*e*	*e*	*e*
h	*h*	*h*	*h*
r	*r*	*r*	*r*
t	*t*	*t*	*t*
b	*b*	*b*	*b*
i	*i*	*i*	*i*
m	*m*	*m*	*m*

Page 11

1	2	3
abcd	stuv	ijkl

4	5	6
qrst	efgh	mnop

Page 13

pie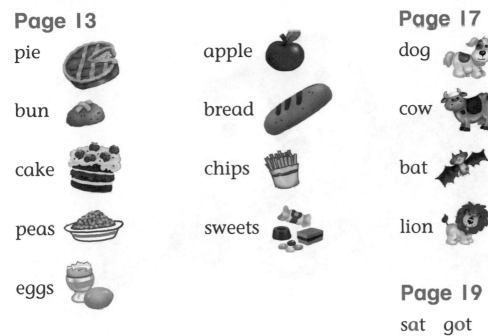

bun

cake

peas

eggs

apple

bread

chips

sweets

Page 15

1. "I hid it by the <u>pans</u>."
2. "They make me <u>mad</u>."
3. <u>Dad</u> bit <u>back</u>, then hit the <u>cat</u>.
4. It <u>span</u> round ten times just like a <u>fan</u>.
5. <u>Sam</u> and <u>Jan</u> looked <u>sad</u>.
6. "<u>Dad</u>! <u>Dad</u>! It is very <u>bad</u>!"
7. Out of it <u>sprang</u> a very strange <u>rat</u>.
8. He <u>slammed</u> the <u>van's</u> doors.

Page 17

dog

cow

bat

lion

fox

bear

hippo

pig

Page 19

sat got man hope
flat stop lad happy

Page 21

1. a cap or hat
2. Jan
3. red
4. the van
5. the big cat
6. pats

23

Published 2004

Letts Educational, The Chiswick Centre,
414 Chiswick High Road, London W4 5TF
Tel 020 8996 3333   Fax 020 8996 8390
Email mail@lettsed.co.uk
www.letts-education.com

Text, design and illustrations © Letts Educational Ltd 2004
Nelson handwriting font © Thomas Nelson

Book Concept, Development and Series Editor:
Helen Jacobs, Publishing Director
Author: Clive Gifford
Book Design: Linda Males
Illustrations: Rikki O'Neill

British Library Cataloguing in Publication Data

A CIP record for this book is available from the British Library.

ISBN 978-1-84315-417-4

Printed in Italy

Colour reproduction by PDQ Digital Media Limited, Bungay, Suffolk